Lights, Camera, Love

EMMA BRAY

Chapter One

Katie

I started not to take this job, but my agent was so insistent, and she's right, I know. I might already be one of the most well-known faces on the big screen, but this movie is going to be a big deal. It's going to be one of those roles that makes my career. I could be remembered forever for this performance.

It's got a bit of everything. Drama, a touch of comedy, romance. Not too serious but not too silly. It's the whole package. The kind of role that actors and actresses kill for, yet the producers specifically asked for me.

I initially squealed and jumped at the opportunity, but I quickly deflated like a popped balloon when my agent told me who my costar would be.

Justin Robison. Notorious Hollywood playboy. America's heartthrob. Bad boy extraordinaire.

His reputation precedes him. He's known for sleeping with every young costar he's ever had. Scandal seems to follow him everywhere he goes. While some people say any publicity is good publicity, I don't want any of that negative sort of attention.

I'm America's sweetheart. I'm known for being the good girl, the wholesome girl, and I want to keep it that way.

So, I started not to take this job to avoid working with Justin. But as my agent pointed out, I've never actually met the guy, so it's not really fair for me to judge him too harshly without even knowing him. And that's true, I guess. As someone in the entertainment business myself, shouldn't I know better than anyone that you can't believe everything you read in the tabloids?

So here I am, ready to give this a shot. I'm not going to lie, though. I'm wary as hell. We're already ten minutes past time to start shooting, and everything is still on hold because my costar hasn't shown up yet, and apparently, we can't begin without him since he's in the opening scene.

It's not looking good.

I let out a frustrated sigh and glance over at the director who looks fit to be tied. He's on the phone with someone—Justin's agent probably—his face red as a beet as he curses and threatens that he better "get his ass here pronto or else."

Honestly, though, even I know the threats are meaningless. A name like Justin's is so big he can get away with crap like this. Technically, I probably could too, but I make it a point to always be on time to everything. I'm known for my excellent work ethic and calm demeanor. I'm easy to work with and never a diva.

Unfortunately, it looks like Hollywood's

heartthrob is going to be a prima donna and a half.

Great. Just great. I have to fight to keep from rolling my eyes. Instead, I bounce my leg up and down nervously, an anxious habit I have a hard time breaking when I'm left waiting.

I tried to come into this with an open mind, giving Justin a clean slate, but I have to admit, he's not making the best first impression showing up late right off the bat.

That's what I think anyway.

Until the man walks through the door.

You know how in the movies when a hot guy walks in, the camera slows and everything seems to move in super slow motion as he tosses his head, his perfect hair tousling with the slight movement?

Yeah, it's like that.

I've seen Justin in the papers before, so of course I know what he looks like, but nothing could have prepared me for the full-frontal impact of the man in the flesh.

He's a god. It's as simple as that. He has rakishly good looks with his dark hair and strong, chiseled jawline that's sporting that perfect amount of stubble that's not messy-looking but sexy.

He has a devil may care attitude. You can tell it in his stance. And he's even taller than he appears on TV and in the papers. The man has to be at least six foot four. I'm no munchkin at five foot seven myself. I'm not the tallest girl in the world, but I'm certainly not the shortest either.

But what sends my heart racing is when his smoldering brown eyes, eyes that look as sinful and addictive as chocolate lock onto me.

It's like the world falls away. I can't fully describe the feeling that washes over me at being the object of his intense scrutiny. And intense is the only way to describe it. Yeah, guys look at me all the time. I get checked out everywhere I go.

But no one has ever looked at me like this. His eyes are piercing, like he's trying to probe right into my soul.

It leaves me shaken when I finally break eye contact with him to look down at my phone again. I'm trying to act like he doesn't affect me so much, but my hands are trembling, and I know my face is flushed.

Oh god, this is going to be a disaster. There's no way I can act alongside this man.

I've completely chickened out. I'm uncrossing my legs to stand and walk out of this studio right now, but a shadow passes over me, and I look up to find him towering over me. He's still staring at me with those smoldering eyes of his, and I feel my knees go weak.

What the hell is wrong with my body? Stupid body! I'm furious at it for betraying me like this.

"Everyone out!" he barks to the room, his eyes still pinned on me.

Everyone freezes, and then the director gives an incredulous laugh. "Are you serious?" he asks Justin, the screenplay in one hand and the other hand on his hip.

Justin finally turns away from me long enough to glance at the director. "Did I stutter?" he tosses at him nonchalantly.

The director sputters before his face turns red and he finally begins mumbling under his breath as he gathers up some more papers and then makes a motion for everyone to clear the room.

"You've got five minutes," he says sternly to Justin before he leaves.

Justin doesn't acknowledge him. His sole focus is back on me.

And I'm just sitting there stupefied at everything that just happened, staring back up at him like a deer caught in the headlights.

What in the ever loving fuck is happening?

Justin

Breathtaking. Gorgeous. Beautiful. *Mine.*

Those are the thoughts passing through my head as soon as I lay eyes on the blonde-haired, blue-eyed angel sitting on one of the tall, barstool-style chairs set out around the studio.

I have to confess that I didn't even know who I'd be working with today when I showed up to set late. I didn't even take the time to go over the notes my agent sent me about who my costar would be.

Hell, I haven't even looked at the script.

It's not that I don't care about my job. It's just become routine. And it's not like I can't memorize the script in under five minutes, thanks to my photographic memory.

Of course I know who Katie Edwards is. America's sweetheart. She's glamorous on the red carpet, but she still somehow retains that adorable girl next door look.

Sexy as sin yet still innocent-looking.

Every man's wet dream.

I'm around beautiful women all the time. It comes with the territory.

But no other fellow celebrity's presence has ever affected me like this. My heart has never jumped into my throat the first time I laid eyes on someone in the flesh. My pulse has never thundered in my ears like this.

I've never before had the insane urge to toss a girl over my shoulder and march her straight back home with me and keep her all to myself.

I want to learn every fucking thing there is to know about Katie Edwards.

She's younger than me by at least ten years, but ask me if I give a fuck.

Her eyes are still locked with mine as the room clears out. I'm probably being rude as hell, but I can't stop staring at her.

I feel like I'll die if I don't look at her.

She's breathtakingly beautiful with her slim body and long legs, her hair that goes all the way down to her waist in soft waves, her pink, bee-stung lips, her baby blue eyes framed by thick lashes.

But it's more than that. There's a purity about her, something real and unsullied. A light seems to shine out of her eyes.

She seems sweet, non-calculating, something that is so hard to find in females in this business. Most of them are out for blood, always trying to claw their way to the top, looking for opportunities. I of all people ought to know, I can't help thinking wryly.

I don't get any of those kinds of vibes from this sweet girl sitting in front of me, though.

She's staring up at me warily like I've lost my mind.

And maybe I have.

"Katie Edwards," I say her name slowly as I take another step toward her chair. The scent of her shampoo, something flowery, wafts up to my nostrils, and I inhale deeply. I stuff my hands in my pockets to keep her from seeing how I ball them into fists to repress the urge to reach out and touch her. No need to act like a total psycho and scare her right off the bat.

"I'm..." I start to introduce myself, but she interrupts me.

"Justin Robison," she pushes herself up from the chair and takes a step back, putting the chair between us. I frown at the new distance, irrationally bothered by it. "Yeah, I know who you are. There was no need to clear the room to introduce yourself. You're already late, and now we're holding the whole production team up." She crosses her arms as she looks up at me.

I blink at her candid tone, slightly taken aback. I'm not used to actresses berating me. Quite the opposite, actually. I usually have to fight them off when they throw themselves at me whether I want them or not. I'm not saying that in a conceited manner either. It's actually quite tiresome.

Ironic that the one woman I wouldn't mind throwing herself at me seems to be doing nothing but trying to distance herself from me.

I try to shrug it all off with a smile and a reassuring, "Clive will live. He and I have worked together before." It's true. The director is very familiar with how I operate, which is usually by flying by the seat of my pants but whatever. I might be late sometimes. I might have a 'fuck it' attitude. But at the end of the day, I still deliver. It's why I keep getting cast for movies time and time again.

"Katie," I taste her name again and take another step toward her. I don't know why. I don't know what I'm planning to do. God only knows how much I want to taste her lips, run my fingers through her hair, feel the velvety softness of her skin.

Just fucking be near her.

"Justin," she parrots my name back at me

and takes a step back. A shiver runs down my spine at my name coming from her lips. I want to hear her moaning it in my ear as I...

"Time's up!" Clive announces as he strolls back into the room, glaring at me before his eyes flick between Katie and me.

I glare back at him, pissed beyond measure at being interrupted. From what I don't know. It's not like we were even doing anything. I just want to talk to her. Get to know her.

She turns to walk away from me, and I panic. I reach out and grab her wrist to stop her from leaving.

She gasps as she turns back to face me, her hair bouncing around her face at the movement.

Electricity snaps along every nerve ending in my body at finally touching her. Her skin is just as velvety soft as I imagined it would be.

She feels so fucking delicate. A surge of protectiveness swells up within me.

Mine.

Everything about this girl is screaming

she's mine. I don't know how I know that, but I do.

Her eyes flick down to where I'm holding her wrist, and then she looks up at me and attempts a scowl.

But I feel her pulse thundering under my grip. I feel the slight tremor that goes through her. She feels this too. This whatever this is between us.

I can't help but tighten my grip on her as I lean down and say right into her ear. "This isn't over, Katie. We'll talk more later."

Her scent surrounds me, and I have to fight from nuzzling into her hair right there in front of everyone. Instead, I inhale, like a wolf scenting its mate, before I finally rise to my full height and release her.

"I'm aware of your, ah," she stumbles over her words, her cheeks prettily flushed before she settles on, "reputation." She covers her wrist where I was holding her as if trying to wipe away the contact, "And nothing is going to happen between us," she hisses at me before promptly turning and striding away over to where the director and other staff are.

I stare after her, dumbfounded, though

why I don't know. I'm well aware of what the tabloids print about me. No matter that half of it isn't even true. I usually don't give a fuck one way or the other if people believe the trash printed in them.

But the thought that Katie might really believe me to be the unfeeling Hollywood player that the tabloids paint me as stings. It bothers me more than I care to admit.

I square my jaw as I follow her onto the set.

I determine right then and there that I'm going to do everything I can to show her I'm not that guy from the papers.

Because whether Katie Edwards realizes it or not, I've learned one truth this morning.

That she's mine. Everything about her tells me so whether she realizes it or not. And nothing will stand in my way of having her. Not even the woman herself.

Chapter Two

Katie

Justin is relentless. Each day after filming he begs me to go out with him. He sends flowers to my dressing room every day.

No matter how many times I shoot him down, he keeps on with dogged determination.

I don't know why he's so persistent. I'm probably just a challenge to him because I'm sure no woman in her right mind has ever said no to him before.

And no matter how much his charming smile makes my knees go weak, no matter how much my heart thumps within my chest when I feel his smoldering gaze on me, no matter how much I might really want to acquiesce to his request, I resist.

I don't want to be another one in the string of his Hollywood conquests.

Nope. No way.

He can smolder on all he wants to. He can look too handsome for his own good with that dark lock of hair that's always falling perfectly over his forehead. His lips can be too sinfully lush for a man. His shoulders can be so perfectly broad and strong-looking.

I'm holding fast.

It's not happening.

Because not only do I not want to be fodder for tomorrow's tabloids, but I also know that if Justin gets me alone, I won't be able to trust myself around him.

I freeze up when it's just me and him, like a mouse caught in a snake's hypnotic stare.

He'd be able to do whatever he wanted with me with little to no opposition from me. I don't think I'd be physically capable of resisting him.

I don't think I'd want to.

And I have my career to think about. My image. I'm known as the good, wholesome girl. The press would have a field day with me being Justin's latest fling. I can see the headlines now. *Hollywood Bad Boy Corrupts America's Sweetheart.*

But it's more than just than that. I've never told anyone this, but I'm still a virgin. I don't know what I'm waiting for. I've been tempted to just give it up and get it over with, but maybe I'm stuck on romantic notions of my first time being special. I'm certainly not experienced enough to be with a Casanova like Justin. I'm sure my lack of experience would be disappointing to him, and I just don't think I could take the humiliation of that. Plus, I don't think I'd be able to handle being another one of his flings or one-night stands. I'm almost certain I would want more, and if he didn't—and he wouldn't because Justin is notoriously known for plowing through women and never committing—it would break me.

So, no matter how persistent my suitor is, no matter how persuasive he may be, no matter how much I deep down might really be tempted to, I cannot allow myself to go out with him.

I just have to get through this job with my reputation still intact.

It's easier said than done, though.

I have to act with Justin every day. I have to commend him on being a professional when he's acting, though. He portrays exactly what he's supposed to for the camera, but I see the intent hidden in his eyes, the intensity he allows to shine through just for me. I'm surrounded by it—by his presence—all day long when we're on set.

He hasn't been late a day since that first day. He's punctual every day—early even, though I know he started showing up early to try to badger me into accepting him.

So, I started showing up just a couple minutes before start time. Me, the girl who is always fifteen minutes early to everything is now coming up right in the nick of time all to avoid one Hollywood rake.

It doesn't help that we spend all day

acting together. It doesn't matter if it's real or not. When we're acting, we're still communicating. So, when I go home at night, his voice, his image is still in my head when I close my eyes.

To make matters worse, our dreaded kiss scene is coming up. I don't know how I'm going to get through it. So far, our characters haven't had to engage in any physical contact. No touching, no kissing, nothing.

Justin hasn't touched me since that first day we met when he grabbed my wrist and practically branded my skin.

I can still feel the imprint of his large hand dwarfing me.

But that's all going to change today. Today, we're slotted to do a big climax scene where his character kisses mine.

Kissing on set isn't a big deal. I've had to do it with plenty of other actors. The first couple of times I did it, it was a bit awkward, but once we become more seasoned professionals, it's just part of the job.

But this is Justin.

Justin. The man who's made it perfectly clear he wants more alone time with me.

Justin. The man who no woman can resist.

I swallow and push my hair back over my shoulder.

I feel eyes burning into me and look up to find Justin's heavy gaze pinned on me.

My cheeks burn at the look on his face.

He can't wait for this scene. It's what he's been waiting for all along.

His eyes are glimmering with intent. He looks like a panther ready to pounce on its prey.

And I'm cornered. I consider running, but I know I can't. This is part of my job. I'm just going to have to get through it.

The director is calling for everyone to get into place on set. Justin crooks his finger at me and motions toward himself in a come hither motion.

The look on his face is smug. I halfway want to slap the smirk off his arrogant face, but I'm more consumed with my ticking heart rate and the slight tremble that's taken over my whole body.

I inhale a shaky breath to try to settle my nerves before I walk onto the set.

It's showtime.

Justin

"Lights! Camera!" My entire body is tense as I wait for Clive to announce the last order in his frame of commands. The one order that will finally give me permission to touch Katie in a way that she won't be able to protest because it's part of our script.

I've been waiting for this moment, counting down the days until we got to this very scene.

The scene that's going to give me an excuse to taste those sweet lips. To truly hold her. Feel that perfect little body pressed up against me.

The look of apprehension on her face lets me know she's been dreading this moment as much as I've been looking forward to it. While maybe that should put me off, I'm not deterred.

No, I've learned something about Katie in all this time of acting with her.

She wants me too. I see the glances she peeks at me. I see the furrow that lines her brow when she catches herself doing it.

She wants me, but she's thinks she's not supposed to.

She's scared of her feelings.

I don't know if it's just because of my reputation or because of something else.

But I plan to tear down every one of those walls today and let her know in no uncertain terms just where I stand.

My begging and pleading and flowers haven't worked. She promptly shoots me down every day when I ask her to spend time with me.

Once I get her in my arms, I'm not going to let her go until she says yes. Until she accepts this wave of energy between us. It's more than chemistry. It's motherfucking explosive.

I don't realize I'm holding my breath until Clive finally yells, "Action!" and I expel it in a rush of air before falling into my role.

It takes every ounce of will I have not to rush through the script to get to the part I've been aching to act out.

Only Katie and I both know it won't be an act when I get her into my arms.

The moment finally arrives, and I probably pull her trembling form into my arms with more gusto than the scene warrants, but fuck, I can't help it. I press her flush against me, her pert little breasts smashed right up against my chest, my arm wrapped around her waist, anchoring her flat stomach against me.

I'm instantly hard at the feeling of her against me, and I know she feels it by the way her eyes widen innocently.

Fuck if that doesn't make precum leak from the tip of my cock.

So sweet. She looks so fucking innocent I don't know if I can take it.

I'm shaking too, my hands trembling as I cup her sweet face. I make no move to hide it from her. I want her to feel everything she does to me.

I want her to see *me*. The real me. Not the me that's been splashed in the tabloids.

Her eyes are as vast and pure as a cloudless sky when she looks up at me. I'm soaring in them. I could stare into them all day and get lost in them.

She's my salvation. I know she is.

I stroke my thumb along her jawline and down over her neck where I feel her pulse fluttering wildly.

And then I lean down and taste her for the first time.

No matter how many times I've fantasized about this moment, nothing could prepare me for the cataclysmic shift that takes place inside my whole body at the feeling of her soft lips underneath mine.

If I wasn't already so certain this girl was meant to be mine, this would do it. Nothing has ever felt so right in my life as this moment right here.

I take my time as I taste her for the first time, taking her bottom lip in a one-lip kiss that I know will translate marvelously on screen. But I'm not even thinking about the damn production right now. That's the furtherest thing from my mind.

Katie. She's all I'm thinking about. Showing her how I feel through this kiss since she won't let me get close enough to her with words.

I feel the moment she lets go of her resistance and surrenders to me, her body melting against my chest.

I tighten my arm around her triumphantly and angle her head up so that I can finally delve inside her mouth.

And holy fuck, she tastes sweeter than anything I've ever tasted before. Like the purest sugar. The finest candy. I'd sell my soul for just one taste.

I kiss her like I want to devour her, and I do. I want to taste all of her. She whimpers under my assault, and the sound is like kryptonite to my ears. I want to see what other sounds she can make.

It takes every ounce of willpower I have to not ravish her right there in front of the whole motherfucking studio—onlookers be damned.

If I didn't abhor the thought of anyone but me seeing her naked body, I just might throw all caution to the wind and do it.

As it is, I'm much too possessive and territorial of this woman to allow anyone else

—man or woman—a glimpse of the treasures hidden beneath her clothing.

That will be for my eyes only.

We stare at each other, both breathing heavily. Her lips are swollen and glistening from our kiss. She looks so damn beautiful I don't know what to do.

There's complete silence for a moment before Clive finally clears his throat and says, "Cut!"

I don't waste any time. No sooner does Clive cut the scene than I grab Katie's hand while she's still in shock over our kiss and pull her with me.

Away from the set, through the double doors, down the vacant hallway, and into the first darkened room I find.

Where we can be alone.

For once, she doesn't resist me.

Chapter Three

Katie

I allow him to pull me along in a daze. Yes, I'm dazed by the kiss Justin just planted on me.

Sweet lord, I've never been kissed like that in my entire life.

Kissed stupid. Senseless. Unable to speak if I wanted to.

Justin pulls me into a room and immediately presses me against the closed door. His body presses completely against mine, and I feel the hardness of his erection pressing against me.

I felt it during that kiss back on set, but my eyes widen ever further now.

Good lord, it feels like it's gotten even bigger.

Too big. He's too big. It would never fit inside my virginal body. That's all my mind keeps chanting even as I feel wetness and a deep throbbing between my legs. I clench my thighs together to try to ease the ache.

The movement doesn't go unnoticed by Justin. His eyes darken, and his tongue comes out to moisten his lower lip.

"Sweet girl," his voice is barely a rasp in my ear as his head lowers to kiss the side of my neck. I hear him inhale deeply, something he seems to do around me a lot. He nuzzles his head into my hair, and I feel his hands fist in it.

"Like silk," he whispers as he runs his fingers through it.

Tingles snap along my scalp at the sensation. It feels so good. If I was a cat, I'd be purring by now.

My head falls to the side, and I can't stop

the mewl that leaves my lips as he continues to lave and suck on the column of my throat.

His hands are moving down my body. They pass over the sides of my breasts, down over my waist and hips, before coming back up to cup my breasts. His thumbs flick over my nipples, which are painfully hard through the thin blouse I'm wearing.

I can't think with him so close, with his lips on me, his hands on me. I don't know where I get the strength, but somehow, I wedge my hands up between our chests and give him a firm push.

Justin is so big and solid there's no way I could really push him away if he didn't allow me to, but thankfully he heeds my signals and takes a step back, his eyes clouded with lust, his breath coming shallowly.

Like mine. I can hear my own pants and feel my frantic pulse galloping away in my chest.

"What is it, Katie?" he asks me earnestly as he steps back toward me to close the distance between us. "What do you need, baby? I'll do anything. Anything you want."

He frowns when I slip away from the

door and put some distance between us. I press my fingertips against my temples. There. Maybe I can think better without him surrounding me, his scent, his body, his masculinity, just *him*.

"Why are you fighting this?" he asks me, his brow furrowed. "I know you can feel this." He motions between us with his hand. He takes another step toward me. "Just give me a chance to show you…"

I cut him off before he can begin his persuasive sweet talking now when my body's defenses are already lowered.

"I don't want to be another one of your conquests, Justin," I tell him truthfully.

He pauses, and then he expels a heavy breath. "Damned motherfucking tabloids," he mutters under his breath before he looks at me dead on. "Katie, what if I told you half the shit those fuckers print about me isn't true?"

I chew on my lip for a moment, but then I see his eyes darken as they fixate on the motion, and I immediately stop. "Maybe all the words aren't true, but the pictures don't lie, Justin. You've been photographed on the arm of almost every woman you've ever worked with. You're known for getting romantically involved with your costars." I look down, somehow feeling bad about accusing him of being a womanizer, even though all the signs point to the fact that he is.

He sighs heavily before he crosses the safe distance I put between us. He breaks down all those barriers all over again when he reaches out to tilt my chin up so I'm forced to meet his eyes.

"I may have gone on a date with many of those women, but that doesn't mean I fucked them."

I flinch at the raw way he says "fuck."

He continues, "The tabloids want to paint me as some sort of player. But it's the women who came onto me most of the time, and most of the time I didn't take them up on more than a date just to placate them because we were working together. I know some of them said we had more together than we did, but they just did it for the publicity."

"But you never denied any of the accusations," I point out.

"No," he shakes his head. "I just let the tabloids print what they wanted, let the women get the publicity they wanted. I didn't want the confrontation." He hangs his head down. "I see now that maybe that was all a mistake."

His eyes are earnest when he lifts his head back up to look at me, "But, Katie, I never thought I would meet someone like you. Someone who I would want to have a good image for. You have to believe me when I tell you I've never felt this way about another woman before in my fucking life."

I can't speak. All I can do is stare up at him with wide eyes, my heart thumping and fluttering with the first wings of hope at his heartfelt words.

He cups my face with his hands. "I promise you, sweet girl, that if you give yourself to me, I won't let anything hurt you. Fuck the tabloids. You'll never be labeled another one of my conquests. I'll tell the world you're my girlfriend. Because that's what I want. You. Mine."

All my resistance falls away, and he must

sense it because he leans in and kisses me again, passionately, insistently.

My arms wind around his neck, and I finally allow my fingers to delve into his mass of raven-black hair.

He groans into my mouth as he slips his hands under my dress. "This fucking dress," he rasps against my mouth. "Do you know how it's taunted me all damn week, watching this red fabric swish and sway on your thighs? How many times I've wanted to rip it off you right there on set?"

I gasp when his fingers slip under my panties and make contact with my bare skin.

He hisses in a breath, "So fucking wet for me, baby. You want this too, don't you, sweet girl?"

He doesn't wait for an answer. He rips my panties from my body and unzips his pants, freeing his huge erection with a groan.

I barely have a chance to glimpse the hard, swollen flesh jutting out from his pants before he lifts me in his arms. My legs circle around him instinctively, and I cling to him as he spins us and pushes my back against the door again.

His lips crash onto mine, effectively rendering me dumb and mute again. I melt into the kiss, loving the feeling of his tongue dancing with mine.

Suddenly, he thrusts his tongue into my mouth at the same time as he rears his hips back and juts his cock straight up into me.

He groans, but my limbs tighten around him, and I scream into his mouth as I feel the barrier of my innocence give way under his quick invasion.

He immediately stills at my distress and pulls back to look down into my eyes questioningly.

I blush as the moment of comprehension dawns on him. "Fucking hell," his eyes are wide. "You're a virgin?"

I bite my lip. "Not anymore," I whisper.

"Fuck, Katie. You should have told me. I'd have been gentler. Fuck," he swears again. "Did I hurt you?" The look on his face is so genuinely worried, I can't help but try to reassure him.

"It did sting, but the pain is fading."

He searches my eyes as if he's trying to make sure I'm telling the truth. He finally drops his forehead down onto mine and takes in a ragged breath. "Fuck, sweet girl. I hate the thought of hurting you, but fuck me if I don't relish the thought that I'm the only man to ever be between these sweet thighs."

My muscles clench around him involuntarily at his possessive words. He makes a choked sound and pushes deeper inside me.

I toss my head back against the door and moan at the delicious sensation. It no longer hurts.

No, it feels so fucking good when he slides inside me. I feel so full, and there's so much pressure. I'm throbbing, aching.

"I know, sweet baby," he whispers against my cheek. "Feels good, doesn't it?" he asks me as he tests me with another gentle prod.

I gasp and tighten my grip on his shoulders. "Yes," I breathe out, my eyes looking up to find his pinned intently on me, watching every emotion flit across my face.

"Fuck, you're so beautiful, Katie." His chocolate eyes are smoldering down at me, and I feel myself go weak. It's a good thing he's holding me in his arms because the way he's looking at me, I'd melt right into a puddle in the floor at his feet were I standing.

I take the initiative for the first time and press my lips against his.

That seems to snap something inside him because he loses control then. He takes command of the kiss, devouring my mouth as he begins to push up inside me insistently. I whimper under the assault of both his mouth and body.

"Oh fuck, Katie, Katie, Katie," he chants against my lips. "Mine. My girl. My sweet, sweet girl." His lips are open against my cheek. His breath fans my ear as he continues to mumble endearments against my skin. I feel my wetness gushing as his thrusts pick up tempo.

"Motherfucker," he grits out, his hips pumping into me furiously, sliding me up and down against the wall. And that pressure, that delicious pressure is building inside me. I can't think. I just need...I need...

"This pussy is mine," he growls out as he continues to stab his thick flesh into me over and over again. "Isn't it?"

I don't realize he really wants an answer

until he slows down, and I let out a cry of distress.

My eyes are wild as I look up at his. "Who's pussy is this, Katie?" he asks me, his own eyes half-crazed with lust.

"Yours," I say breathily, never meaning anything more. It's true. I'm his. I can't ever imagine being with anyone else this way.

"Say my name," he demands, pleads.

I lick my lips, and he groans before leaning down to kiss me again. "Justin," I moan his name against his mouth.

"Good girl," he praises me, his voice deep and husky. "When you come all over my cock, you say my name. You hear me, sweet girl?"

"Oh god!" I call out as I feel every muscle inside me clench.

"Motherfucker!" Justin pants as he stabs jerkily inside me, harder and deeper than before. "Yes, I'm right there with you, baby. Katie, oh, Katie!"

"Justin!" I scream his name as pleasure unlike anything I've ever known blasts through me.

"Fuck yes, baby," he's growling as he

continues to plow into me. Somehow, I feel him getting even harder and larger inside me, and then he's calling out my name as he spills himself into me in a gush of blinding hot heat.

He's smothering my face with kisses, nuzzling my neck, whispering promises in my ear.

How I'm his, how he's going to take care of me, how he's never going to let me go, how he's going to be so good for me, I'll see.

And I believe him.

Chapter Four

Justin

It took every ounce of willpower I had not to take Katie home with me last night and keep her with me.

But she has a reputation to uphold, and I don't want to be the one to ruin it. I know how ruthless people can be in this business and how much one's reputation means in it. As unfair as it is, I know it's more damaging to a female's reputation to be seen as sexually promiscuous than it is a man's. I'm patted on the back for being a supposed player, no matter how untrue the rumors might be.

Katie is known for her wholesome image. The tabloids would have a field day with a good girl like her supposedly going bad.

So, I'm going to do everything within my power to ensure that doesn't happen.

First thing this morning I'm going to announce to the world that she's my girlfriend.

Then, I can take her home with me. I can keep her. I can be with her all the time.

I can't wait to make her publicly mine. Last night without her was torture. Now that I've been inside her, it's the only place I want to be. I don't just want her sleeping next to me, in my arms.

I *need* her. I need her like I've never needed another human being on this planet. She makes everything matter again.

I intend on being early to set again, but I get caught up in traffic. Somehow I stroll onto set just in the nick of time.

My heart is already beating faster at the glimpse I get of my woman. Yes, she's *my* woman, and the world is going to know it today.

My smile falters when she turns to look at me with a crestfallen look on her face.

"Katie?" I ask her cautiously. "What's wrong, baby?"

Other cast members and crew members move away from us, giving us a respectful distance, but I can feel their eyes peeking over at us to watch everything.

Fuck them.

All that matters to me in this moment is my Katie. My sweet girl.

"How could you?" she asks me, her voice breaking with betrayal before she tosses a paper at me and turns on her heels, fleeing the studio.

I'm so stunned all I can do is stare after her as I clutch the paper to my chest. When I finally get my wits back about me enough that I can move, I look down at the paper in my hand.

Hollywood Bad Boy Back at It Again. His Latest Conquest? America's Sweetheart, Katie Edwards. Way to Go, Robison!

My eyes skim incredulously over the article, taking in the trash within. Speculating on how I seduced her, how long it took me, and more of the usual nonsense.

Rage like I've never known fills me. A harsh crinkle sounds out in the totally silent set as I ball the paper up in my fist and fling it away from me with a roar.

I'm feeling murderous. If I could get my hands on the reporter who wrote this trash, their life would be in jeopardy right now. Not over me. I could care less what they print about me.

But the fact that they've hurt Katie. Tarnished her good name. It's unacceptable.

I feel a stab of deep pain at the next thought. Turned her away from me.

I can't fucking breathe. I've got to get out of here. Find her. Tell her this is all a mistake.

Someone must have seen us. Or maybe it was that kiss on set that got some of the other cast members gossiping. One of the tabloid reporters got wind of it, and that's all it took to set the flames in motion. No stopping the wildfire once one of those bloodhounds get the scent.

It doesn't matter how it happened or

who started the rumor. All that matters is that it's out there now, and no matter if I try to say she's my girlfriend now, they'll paint it as her just trying to save face.

How could she think I would do something like this to her? How could she think that after yesterday when I bared my fucking soul to her? After what we shared?

My hands are shaking as I go after her. She's already vacated the building, and I see her in her private car being driven away.

I order my driver to follow her.

I have to explain. I have to fix this.

I can't fucking lose her.

Not when I've just gotten her.

She's my heart, my life, my soul.

Katie

I know Justin followed me home, but I order my bodyguards not to let him past the gate.

I can't see him. I can't talk to him.

I'm too hurt.

Fucking reporters were flooding my

property when I got home. My security team got me in without me having to make a comment.

The crowds eventually dispersed once they saw that I wasn't coming out.

But not him.

Not Justin.

He's as relentless as ever, sitting right outside my gate.

Though what he possibly thinks he could have to say to me that would change anything I don't know.

I don't know how long he plans to sit there, and I don't care.

I can't believe he would do this to me.

He promised me—*promised* me—that I wouldn't be labeled another one of his conquests. Yet the next morning, that's exactly what was plastered all over the papers.

Who did he tell about us? He had to have told someone. How else would the tabloids have known?

It doesn't matter. What matters is that he made me a promise, and he broke it. I can't trust him.

My heart stabs at the remembrance of

him inside me, the possessive words he ground out into my ear while our bodies were one, joined in a way I've never been with anyone else.

But he has, hasn't he? Justin has been with plenty of women. Women who are no doubt way prettier and more experienced than me.

What if it was just sex to him? What if he was just saying what he needed to say to get into my pants? What if all his possessive talk was just that—talk? Things said in the heat of passion, quickly uttered and never remembered.

I cry like I've never cried before because this fucking hurts. It hurts more than anything else I've ever experienced in all my eighteen years.

Justin is nearly thirty years old. He's every woman's fantasy. How stupid was I to think that I, some barely legal virgin, would be able to lock a man like him down?

I don't know how long he sits outside my gate, silently begging entry. I stop looking out the window after the third day.

I don't know what I plan on doing. I

can't seclude myself away from the world forever. I can't keep hiding away like this.

I do know I can't continue on co-starring next to Justin. I've never broken a contract in my life, but I call the director and express my apologies at having to pull out of the film.

He sounds unsurprised and surprisingly sympathetic.

After a week goes by, I get a call from the director.

He sounds nervous when I answer the phone, and for good reason. What he has to tell me has me pissed as hell.

"Katie? Are you sure you can't let bygones be bygones and come finish shooting the film? I tried to honor your wishes and cast someone else to costar alongside Justin, but he refuses to continue shooting the film without you. We're at a complete standstill here."

I hang up without even answering him. Fucking Justin! How dare he! How fucking dare he!

He's the one who broke my heart and made me look like a fool, and he's pinning the entire production on me, like I'm the reason it can't go forward. Because of course Justin fucking Robison isn't replaceable. They could have replaced me with another actress, but they can't replace him, and he's setting an ultimatum that he won't shoot without me.

Well, fuck him. Two can play his game. He's not going to manipulate me into coming near him again by putting the whole production on my shoulders.

I wipe my eyes furiously and call my agent.

Oh, I'm going back to work alright.

Just not with Justin.

Chapter Five

Katie

I show up on set two days later ready to get started on the project I turned down in favor of the one with Justin. Granted, the script isn't as good as the other movie, but whatever.

Maybe Justin will get the message loud and clear that he can't yank me around when he finds out I've moved on and booked another job.

We haven't even started filming yet when suddenly there's a loud bang as the door is thrown open. It slams against the wall, and a seething mad Justin barrels through the door.

His tall, well-defined frame cuts an imposing figure as he stalks over to where I stand next to my new costar, a scowl firmly etched into his face.

His hair is disheveled like he's run his fingers through it over and over again, but he's just as gorgeous as ever in a pair of jeans and a black tee that defines every muscle in his chest. Damn him.

Damn my heart for doing a summersault inside my chest at the sight of him.

"What do you think you're doing?" Justin barks at me as he quickly closes the distance between us.

Despite every instinct in me telling me to step back, I stubbornly stand my ground. I square my shoulders and look up at him like he's a moron. "What does it look like? I'm shooting a new movie."

"Like hell you are," he snaps as his fingers close around my wrist, though not harshly, before he tugs me to him.

Lightning bolts zap through my arm at

the contact, and I see his nostrils flare. I struggle anyway.

"Let me go, Justin," I'm making a scene, but I don't really give a fuck at this point. I can feel the stares of everyone in the room centered on us and the drama unfolding. Hell, this drama is probably more enticing that anything they'd ever see on the big screen.

Justin apparently doesn't care either because he doesn't release me.

"I mean it, Justin. I'm not working with you anymore. I'm shooting *this* film," I state adamantly.

He laughs, but it's not a humorous sound. No, it's devoid of all mirth and filled with warning. He leans in to say directly into my ear where only I can hear, "I've read the script for this movie, Katie. There's no way in hell you're kissing another man on screen ever again."

I didn't even realize there was kissing in this movie, but that's not the point.

"You can't tell me what to do, Justin," I counter back at him, though my voice comes out weaker than I intend.

"Oh yes, I can, sweet girl," his breath fanning my ear is doing things to me. My thoughts are muddling, and I'm not thinking straight. I'm surrounded by his heat, his masculine scent. His eyes are smoldering down at me. "You agreed to be mine, and there's no way in hell I'm sharing you with anyone else—on screen or off."

"You told someone I was just another conquest," I hate myself for how my voice wobbles and how tears prick my eyes.

Justin swears under his breath as his hands come up to cup my cheeks. "Never, baby," he denies adamantly. "I would never do that. I swear. I don't know how that rumor got started, but it wasn't me." He shakes his head and swears again, "Fuck, Katie, you have to believe me. I thought I made it clear how I feel about you. If I didn't, then let me do it now."

My mouth falls open as he falls to one knee before me. A collective gasp comes from everyone in the room as he takes my hand in his and kisses my palm ardently.

My heart begins beating erratically in my chest.

"Katie," he begins, "my sweet girl, my love, my life, I've thought of nothing but you since the first day I saw you on set. I knew then and there you were mine. I know it's fast, but I know when something's right, and, baby, nothing is righter than what we have." He says that last bit adamantly as he kisses my hand again.

"I've been in hell this past week without you. Let me spend the rest of our lives showing you how much you mean to me. Fuck what the tabloids say. Fuck what anyone else says or thinks. All that matters is me and you." He gives my hand a little squeeze as he looks up at me earnestly, pleadingly. Something about having this big man on his knees begging me has me trembling.

"Will you marry me, my sweet girl?" he asks me, his eyes hiding nothing.

I stare down at him, humbled at my feet, unconcerned with how weak he may look. And I finally see it, really see.

The pure, unadulterated love and adoration shining in his eyes. And it takes my breath away that it's for *me*. He really does love me. I'm not just some fling to him.

I let my emotions get in the way of seeing the truth that was right in front of me all along. What's he's been trying to tell me all along.

Justin is just a victim of the tabloids like so many of us celebrities are. I'm suddenly shamed at how I was so quick to discredit him and believe the fodder printed in the papers without ever even giving him a chance to explain.

"I'm sorry," I whisper to him. His face falls, and I quickly fall to my knees in front of him. I place my hands on his face and amend, "No, I mean, I'm sorry for not listening to you. I'm sorry for doubting you," his eyes begin to light up as he anticipates where I'm going with this. "And yes. Yes, I will marry you."

No sooner do I get the words out of my mouth do his lips cover mine.

I vaguely hear clapping and cheering from the people around us.

But none of that matters.

Justin is right.

All that matters is me and him.

Us.

Epilogue

Three Years Later

Justin

"You just wait until we get home, sweet girl," I whisper into my wife's ear as I keep her close, her body pressed securely into the side of mine as we stand on the red carpet together posing for pictures.

A pretty blush tinges her cheeks at my whispered promise, and I can't resist flustering her further. "If I have my way, you'll be pregnant with my twins again."

I married Katie as soon as I could. We had the fastest-planned celebrity wedding in history short of eloping in Vegas. A month later she was already pregnant with our twin girls. I'm shooting for twin boys next time.

And fuck if getting her pregnant isn't my sole mission in life. If I could live with my dick inside her, I would.

But we still have our careers, and they're still booming despite my unusual demands— or perhaps because of them.

Once Katie agreed to marry me, I had it permanently sealed in our contracts that neither of us would do romantic scenes with anyone else. Sure, some people think I'm way too territorial and ridiculously over the top when it comes to my wife, but fuck what they think.

There's no way I can share her, not even if it's not real. I simply can't stomach the thought of another man's hands—or God forbid his lips—on my sweet girl. Nor do I want another woman's on me ever again.

The tabloids have finally given up on me.

Now that they see I'm a happily married man who won't give another woman a spare glance, much less the time of day, they've moved on to another victim for their vicious rumors.

Everyone knows without a shadow of a doubt that I adore my wife. Most importantly, she finally knows it. Thank God.

My eyes rove over her in her floor-length red dress. Fuck, but she's still the most stunning woman I've ever laid eyes on with her sparkling blue eyes and blonde hair. An angel. So pure. Still so innocent-looking despite the despicable, filthy things I do to her behind closed doors.

I'm fighting a hard-on all night, feeling the bare skin of her back underneath my hand as I lead her through the motions of what we must both go through.

And when we both get an award for the latest film we starred in together, I kiss her on stage for everyone to see. She's still my favorite costar, and our chemistry is so off the charts, producers are lining up to book us to star in films together.

She's perfect. My other half. I love the life

we've built together. I love working with the love of my life. She shares my passion for acting. We have two beautiful little girls.

The night finally ends, and I'm practically sprinting us to where our limo is waiting to carry us home.

No sooner do we get into the back of the limo do I have her in my lap, her legs straddling me. "Fuck, baby. I can't wait," I groan, feeling the moisture already beading up on the head of my cock. I pull her down and grind myself against her. She gasps, throwing her head back.

I take advantage of the movement to lean in and kiss the column of her throat.

I love her neck. I love marking her with my bites and sucks. I don't give a fuck that it distresses the makeup artists to no end. They can cover it up, but I'd rather she wear my hickeys for the whole world to see.

To remind everyone who she belongs to.

Her tiny hands fist in my hair as she accepts me biting and sucking on her neck. "Justin," she moans my name, a sound I never tire of.

I continue to feast on her until suddenly

she pulls back from me.

I start to protest, but all sounds die in my throat when she drops to her knees in front of me and I realize her intent.

Oh, fuck, yes.

She gives me a mischievous look as she unzips my pants and releases my throbbing erection. It pops up in the air, the tip purple and swollen and leaking.

She licks her lips, and I almost come right there on the spot.

"Katie, please don't tease me, baby," I growl. "I've wanted you all night. I warn you I'm not going to last long."

She smiles up at me impishly before her tongue flicks out and tentatively laps the bead of moisture from my head. Another one surges up instantly to replace it. I can't stop the groan that tears from my throat at just that lightest brush of her tongue.

Thankfully, she doesn't tease me any more than that because the next thing I know she plunges her mouth on me, deep throating me to the hilt.

"Fuck!" I roar, my hands fisting into her

hair, making a mess of her fancy updo. I almost come right then and there.

I don't know what I like better. Her tight little pussy or her hot little mouth. My wife's got it all.

She bobs up and down on me, hollowing her cheeks, sucking and twirling her tongue on my tip until I can't take it anymore.

"You've gotten too good at that," I rasp down at her. I was pleased as fuck to find out that her mouth was just as virginal as her pussy. No other cock has ever nor will ever be between her lips but mine.

As much as I love to come in her mouth, though, I meant what I said before about getting her pregnant again.

I jerk her up onto my lap and pull her down onto my aching length, impaling her on me as I push up deep into her.

My eyes damn near roll back in my head at the sensation of her tight, wet heat sheathing me.

I feel her rippling around me, and she moans deeply. I smirk, and my cock jerks within her at the knowledge that she's coming on my cock already.

"My sweet girl loves that's cock, doesn't she? Already milking me, aren't you, sweet girl? Just begging for your man to dump his load all up in you, aren't you?"

"Oh god, Justin!" she screams as I stab up into her quickly.

My breath is coming out in ragged puffs. I feel my balls tightening up already. I wasn't lying to her. I'm not going to last long. I've been wound up too long watching her in that red dress all night. Fuck, I love her in red.

I pump up into her once, twice, three more times before I feel myself begin to boil over.

"Oh fuck, here it comes baby. Just for you, sweet girl. Oh fuck, Katie!" My spine tingles, and then I feel the pressure blast up my stalk before it spurts out of my head and sprays deep into my wife's womb.

I jet stream after stream of cum into her, my balls drawing up almost painfully with my release.

I feel her pussy quaking and spasming around me, only intensifying my pleasure.

Fuck, she's perfect.

Katie slumps forward in my arms, and I

savor the feeling of her breasts pressed against my chest.

I keep my cock seated inside her as I cradle her against me, thankful with everything in me for the woman in my arms.

"I love you, sweet girl," I kiss the top of her head, this woman who's mine to cherish.

"I love you too, Justin."

It doesn't matter how many awards I win, how many fans I have. Nothing compares to hearing those words from my wife's lips.

THE END

Connect with Emma!

Visit Emma's website to get a FREE book you can't get anywhere else: www.authorem mabray.com.

9 798215 151785